GWENDOLYN'S PET GARDEN

ANNE RENAUD   illustrated by RASHIN KHEIRIYEH

 Nancy Paulsen Books

To Emma, who always wanted a pet —A.R.

To all who try to see out of the box
and compromise to reach their goals and bring
happiness to themselves and others —R.K.

NANCY PAULSEN BOOKS

An imprint of Penguin Random House LLC, New York

Text copyright © 2021 by Anne Renaud
Illustrations copyright © 2021 by Rashin Kheiriyeh

Nancy Paulsen Books is a trademark of Penguin Random House LLC.

Visit us online at penguinrandomhouse.com

Library of Congress Cataloging-in-Publication Data
Names: Renaud, Anne, 1957– author. | Kheiriyeh, Rashin, illustrator.
Title: Gwendolyn's pet garden / Anne Renaud; illustrated by Rashin Kheiriyeh.
Description: New York: Nancy Paulsen Books, [2021] | Summary: "Gwendolyn begs
her parents for a pet, and soon discovers how much she loves taking
care of her very own garden"—Provided by publisher.
Identifiers: LCCN 2020019292 | ISBN 9781984815286 (hardcover) |
ISBN 9781984815309 (ebook) | ISBN 9781984815293 (ebook)
Subjects: CYAC: Gardening—Fiction. | Pets—Fiction.
Classification: LCC PZ7.R28443 Gw 2021 | DDC [E]—dc23
LC record available at https://lccn.loc.gov/2020019292

Manufactured in China by RR Donnelley Asia Printing Solutions Ltd.
ISBN 9781984815286
1 3 5 7 9 10 8 6 4 2

Design by Suki Boynton
Text set in Boucherie Flared
The art was drawn in pencil, crayon, and ink and colored
in watercolor, gouache, oil, and collages.

Gwendolyn Newberry-Fretz wanted a pet.
More than polka-dotted rain boots.
More than a telescope.
More than anything.

Gwendolyn grouched and pouted. Pestered and pleaded. Argued and bartered. But Gwendolyn's parents simply would not budge. Certainly not for a pet with two legs.

Can I have a cockatoo?
Can I have a toucan?
Can I have a macaw?

"Birds throw feathery fits," said Father.

Under no circumstances for a pet with four legs.

Can I have a gerbil?
Can I have a hedgehog?
Can I have a chinchilla?

"Fur makes my nose sneeze," said Mother.

And never in a million years for a pet
with eight or ten legs.

Can I have a tarantula?
Can I have a lobster?
Can I have a crab?
Can I have a shrimp?

"Spiders give me nightmares," said Father.
"Shellfish give me hives," said Mother.

"I want a pet to keep me company," said Gwendolyn.
"You have us," said her parents.
"I want a pet to teach it tricks," said Gwendolyn.
"Your little brother fetches and rolls over," said her parents.

"I want a pet to care for," said Gwendolyn.

"Well . . . ," said her parents.

"You can take care of this!"

"It's a box of dirt," said Gwendolyn.

"It's a bed of soil," said her parents.

"It smells of swamp,"
said Gwendolyn.
"It smells of possibilities,"
said her parents.

So Gwendolyn started digging.
But all she found was more dirt, a dead beetle,
and a peculiar piece of root.

"Are you growing frustrated?"
asked her parents.

"I'm sprouting an idea,"
said Gwendolyn.

Gwendolyn went to the library and
borrowed *The Great Book of Gardening*.
She became savvy about soil,
seeds, sunlight, and shade.

And when Gwendolyn had read all she
could, she borrowed seeds from the seed
lending library. She even offered to trade
them for her marbles and seashell collection,
but the librarian said the seeds were free.

Gwendolyn made rows of little holes in the soil
and sprinkled them with marigold seeds . . .

basil and fennel seeds . . .
and finally, zucchini seeds.

Then she filled the holes up, giving each one
a pat of encouragement and a splash of water.

She crossed her fingers and toes
and whispered, "Please grow."

Some days, the soil needed more watering.
Other days, it soaked up the sun.

And when Pickle tried to bury his bone in the soil,
Gwendolyn told him to bury it in his own backyard.

But still, nothing happened.

Until the day the soil did a trick. It pushed
up two tiny leaves that slowly unfolded and
turned their faces to the sun.

Then the soil did more tricks. More leaves peeked out,
sniffed the air, and stretched upward on thin stems.

The stems budded!
The buds bloomed!
Vines and tendrils like hairs of
wild beasts inched along the soil,
and delicate shoots of
fennel and basil
scented the air
with a peppery
licorice perfume.

Gwendolyn's
Garden

Gwendolyn named the plants.

She studied them daily, measuring each one as it grew, and recorded the changes in her notebook.

The bed of soil was now carpeted with fiery marigolds, blossoming zucchinis, and herbs that shimmied in the wind. It fluttered with butterflies and bees and sang with the chirps of cicadas and crickets.

It did not have two legs, four legs, or any legs
at all. But it was *alive*, and Gwendolyn could
talk to it, care for it, and watch it grow.

GROWING YOUR PET GARDEN

Did you know that more and more children are discovering the joy of gardening? It helps you learn all sorts of things: the life cycle of plants, responsibility for their care and nurturing, as well as an increased awareness of where food comes from.

There is a lot to consider when making your garden. But that is all part of the fun!

Where should you plant your garden? What plants should you choose, and when should you plant them?

Some plants grow quicker than others. Some need more light. Some require more care than others. And some—like, snow peas, radishes, and cherry tomatoes—can even be snacked on as they grow. How cool is that!

Your garden could even have a theme, like a rainbow garden, a pizza garden, or a salad garden. A rainbow garden could have flowers and vegetables in every color of the rainbow. A pizza or salad garden could have pizza toppings, like tomatoes and basil, or salad ingredients, like lettuce and chives. You could even plant the seeds in concentric circles.

So once you have decided what to grow, where do you go for seeds? Hardware stores and garden centers are a very good start. Gwendolyn got her seeds from a seed lending library. Are you familiar with those? If not, here is the scoop.

Before computers were used to help people find books in libraries, information on each library book was recorded on a small card. These cards were kept in a card catalog cabinet that often looked like this.

© Anne Renaud

Most libraries no longer need these cabinets. So what are they doing with them? They've converted them into seed lending libraries.

A seed library is a collection of seeds that can be "borrowed" for free. It operates on the honor system, meaning that it relies on the honesty of the people who use it. Patrons of a library take the seeds and plant them. Then, at the end of the growing season, borrowers are encouraged to return some of their newly cultivated seeds to the library so others can use them. This keeps the library well stocked and creates a culture of sharing and sustainability.

If there is no seed lending library where you live, why not encourage your library or community to set up their own?

Happy gardening!